The Pitt Street
Pirates

TERRY DEARY

With illustrations by
Stefano Tambellini

Barrington Stoke

First published in 2004 in Great Britain by
Barrington Stoke Ltd
18 Walker Street, Edinburgh, EH3 7LP

www.barringtonstoke.co.uk

This edition first published 2015

Text © 2004 Terry Deary
Illustrations © 2015 Stefano Tambellini

A CIP catalogue record for this book is available
from the British Library upon request

ISBN: 978-1-78112-468-0

Printed in China by Leo

Contents

Chapter 1
A Pitt Street Plan

Roger Redbeard didn't have a red beard.

"Why are you called Redbeard then?" Sniffle Smith, his weedy friend, asked.

"Because all my family are called Redbeard," Roger told him. "Why are you called Sniffle?"

"Dunno," Sniffle sniffed. "*Sn-Sn-Sn-iff*! Was your dad called Redbeard?"

Roger put a hand on his thick *black* hair. "I never met my dad," he said.

"So, does your *mum* have a red beard?" Sniffle asked.

Roger gave a sigh. Sniffle was as thick as they come. "The Redbeards took their name from Captain Redbeard. He was a great pirate!" Roger said with pride.

"What sort of planes did he fly?" Sniffle asked.

"P-I-R-A-T-E. Pirate, you dummy! Not pilot!" Roger said. "The terror of the high seas. Robber of Spanish gold."

Sniffle gave a sigh. "I wish we were pirates. I'd like to find some gold."

Roger looked hard at the shabby houses across the street. He closed his eyes … and saw them in his mind as great ships.

Galleons under full sail. "Why not, Sniffle? Why not?"

"Er ... is it that we haven't got a ship?" Sniffle asked.

"We'll build one! Mr Clark at the corner shop has stacks of old wooden boxes! We'll build a ship and sail the seven seas."

"But I have to be back in time for supper," Sniffle said.

"Then we'll sail the seven lakes of Pitt Street Park!" Roger shouted and jumped to his feet. He ran down the street to the corner shop. Sniffle walked slowly after him.

Out of some dark corner came a cat. A skinny, flea-bitten cat with one ear missing. They called her Minnie.

Roger Redbeard was the first of his family for 400 years to build a pirate ship. And the first one ever to build it in his back yard at number 7 Pitt Street. Sniffle sniffed when he saw it.

"It'll never float!"

"Hah! That's what they said about the *Titanic*!" Roger said, with a grin.

"Did they?" asked Sniffle.

"They did! And look where the *Titanic* ended up!" he said.

"I see!" Sniffle smiled – but he didn't see. He still felt unhappy. "Can I be Captain?" he asked.

"You can be Cabin Boy," Roger told him. "You can go up into the crow's nest up top and keep a look out."

"Is that a big job?"

"You can't get any higher." Roger grinned.

After hours of hard work the boat was ready. There were just one or two problems.

"How do we get it down to the lake?" asked Sniffle.

"What a stupid thing to ask," Roger replied. "How do they get a ship in a bottle?"

"I don't know," said Sniffle.

"Well, there you are!" Roger cried.

"But it won't go through the gate!" Sniffle said.

"It came in, didn't it?" Roger grinned again.

But Sniffle was right.

"Push!" the Captain told him. Sniffle pushed. The boat didn't move. "You push and I'll pull!" Roger told him.

The Cabin Boy pushed one end and the Captain pulled the same end. The boat didn't

move. Captain Redbeard stroked his chin – with no red beard on it. "We need more help," he said. "And I know just where to get it!"

Roger set off up the steps and along the hall to Flat 13.

Chapter 2
A Mighty Mate

In Flat 13, Ellie was lying on her bed. It
was a huge bed. Ellie was a big girl. She
was reading a book and watching an old
black-and-white film. She was clever like
that – she could do two things at once.

Sniffle could never do two things at once.

Ellie heard the rap at the door. "Come in!"
she called.

Roger kicked the door open. Crack.

"Roger!" Ellie cried and gave him a hug. "You don't know how long I've waited for this moment," she sighed.

"What moment?" Roger blinked.

"Why, the moment when you walked in here just to see me. What do you want, darling?" she asked gently.

"He wants some fish," Sniffle said.

"I'm Captain Roger Redbeard. And I need help to get my new ship into the water," Roger told her.

Ellie jumped off the bed. "Oh, are you playing at pirates? Can I join the crew?"

"Not playing," Roger said. "And you don't get women pirates."

"Yes, you do. There's one in the opera, *The Pirates of Penzance*. She's called Ruth," Ellie said at once.

"Well," Roger said, "my crew of pirates are going to be Ruth-less. Hee! Hee! Hee! Get it? Ruth-less!"

Sniffle smiled. But he didn't get the joke.

"OK, but then you don't get your ship in the water," Ellie said with a shrug.

"You're in the crew," Roger said at once. "First Mate."

"She could have my job in the cow's nest," Sniffle offered.

"Crow's nest," Roger hissed.

"Just as you say."

"No. She wouldn't fit."

Ellie led the way to the door. "Avast and belay there!" she cried. (She'd read the right pirate books.)

"Er, how do I do that?" Sniffle asked.

Roger gave a shrug and went into the yard with Ellie.

Ellie looked at the ship. "It'll never float," she said sadly.

Sniffle smiled. What had Roger told him? "That's what they said about the *Titanic*! And look where it ended up!"

"At the bottom of the sea," said Ellie. "It hit an iceberg."

There was no reply to that. Sniffle sniffled. *Sn-Sn-Sn-iff*!

Roger looked at Ellie. He was cross. "Are you going to say it won't go through the gate?" he snapped.

"Yeah," the Cabin Boy cut in. "Well, how do they get bottles in ships? Eh?"

Ellie smiled. "Never mind. It can go over the wall." And she picked up the galleon and carried it towards the street. Roger put a hand under the ship. "OK, Ellie, I've got it!"

Ellie lifted the ship onto the top of the wall and ran through the gate to catch it as it slid into the back lane. Then she marched off towards Pitt Street Park. The Captain, the

Cabin Boy and the skinny cat went running after her.

Small kids rushed to their doors to look at the splendid sight. A galleon in full sail down Pitt Street!

"What are you going to call her, Roger?" Mr Clark called out as the ship passed the corner shop.

Roger had a quick think. "Er ... the *Titanic!*" he called back.

Old Mr Clark shook his head. "Hope there are no icebergs down on the park pond."

There were no icebergs. But there were lots of kids with sailboats and motorboats of all shapes and sizes.

When the Pitt Street Pirates and the *Titanic* got to the edge of the pond, the kids ran away to hide in the bushes as if they'd

seen a mad dog. Soon the pond was empty.
Ellie slid the ship onto the grass at the edge of
the pond.

"How's that, Captain?" she asked.

Roger gave a shrug. "Not bad. But you didn't have to carry it all the way. Sniffle and I could have done it on our own, you know."

"Aye, aye, Captain," Ellie said in a humble voice.

Roger Redbeard patted his ship with pride. "I name this ship *Titanic*. Er ..."

"May God bless her and all who sail in her," Ellie added.

"I was just going to say that," Roger snapped. "May dogs get her and all who fail in her!" He gave the ship a great push to send her sliding into the cruel sea.

Sniffle cheered.

Minnie the cat purred.

Ellie clapped.

But the *Titanic* didn't budge. She had made up her mind to stay on the shore.

Chapter 3
A Treasure Island

Fifty kids were watching from the bushes in Pitt Street Park as Ellie stepped up to the galleon and pushed her gently towards the water. Fifty kids were silent as the *Titanic* hit the water with a splash. Fifty kids and Ellie and a cat gasped as the ship bobbed happily up and down on the water.

"It floats!" Ellie said.

Roger gave a shrug and tried not to look too pleased. "What did you think it would do?" he asked.

"Float, Captain," said Ellie and grinned. "Shiver me timbers."

"Er ... shiver your what?" asked Roger.

"Me timbers, Captain. That's what all the pirates say," Ellie told him.

"Do they?" Roger blinked. "You seem to know a lot about it."

"I've read all the books, seen all the films. I know all about pirates!" she told him.

"Uh-huh? Anything else you think I should know about them?"

"Don't worry. I'll tell you all at the pirates' den tonight."

"Pirates' den?" Sniffle cut in.

"That's right. My room," Ellie went on happily. "Ship's biscuits and grog!"

"I don't like frogs," Sniffle said.

Roger just shook his head. This pirate stuff was a lot harder than he'd thought. "All aboard the *Titanic*!" he cried, and he stepped off the bank onto the swaying ship.

Sniffle followed. He had a hard time getting up to the crow's nest at the top of the mast. The mast was weak and it swayed a bit.

The ship sank a little lower in the water as Ellie joined them with a cry of, "Shiver me timbers!"

Minnie the cat jumped on board just as Ellie pushed them off from the shore with a bit of wood. She used it to paddle them out

into the lake. Roger grabbed the rudder and tried to steer.

Roger closed his eyes. Now he could see the seven seas ahead of them. "Tiver me shimbers!" he yelled. He looked up to the top of the mast. "Can you see anything, Mr Cabin Boy?" he cried.

Sniffle pointed back to the shore. "A Spanish galleon, Captain!" he called back.

Roger swung round. There, on the shore, was a little girl. She stood and glared at them. She had on the most white and frilly dress Roger had ever seen.

"I say! You people in that boat! Come here at once!" she ordered.

"Turn the ship around and go back, Ellie!" Roger said.

"You mean avast and belay, don't you?" the First Mate asked.

"Do I?" the dazed Captain replied.

"Aye, aye, Sir!" Ellie cried and paddled back to the shore.

Roger stared at the girl who stood there. She had small blue bows in her hair. But he wasn't looking at her hair. He was looking at her bike. It was a three-wheeler and it glittered like a galleon full of gold.

The *Titanic* bumped up against the shore and Sniffle fell into the lake. "Help! Roger! Help! I can't swim. Help! I'm drowning!" Sniffle wailed.

"No, you're not," Ellie said, with a sigh. "The water's only up to your knees. Stand up, Cabin Boy."

Sniffle gave a silly grin and dripped his way out of the lake.

"Now," the girl on the golden bike said, "I want you to take me out to the island in the middle of the lake on your boat."

Roger just gazed at her and Sniffle just grinned. Ellie looked angry. "Why should we?" she said.

The little girl tossed her curls and said, "Because I'm Ruby Rose."

"I'm sorry to hear that," Sniffle said.

"My daddy is the mayor of this town, Mayor Rupert Rose," Ruby went on. "The town golf club is having a Fun Day for children. It's my job to sort out the treasure hunt."

"Treasure!" Roger said, all excited.

"I plan to hide a clue on that island in the lake," Ruby told them. "So take me across in that raft of yours."

"Yes, Miss," Roger said.

"No way," Ellie snapped.

"Wait a moment," Roger said to Ellie. "I am the Captain."

"Sorry, Sir," Ellie said in a low voice. "But we can make some money out of this. She'll have to pay us!"

Roger looked even more excited. "Yeah!" he said to Ruby. "It'll cost you ten pence ..."

"A pound!" Ellie said.

"OK!" Ruby Rose said. "I'll pay you when we're safely back."

And they set off across the lake again, with Miss Ruby Rose aboard.

The Pitt Street Pirates sailed in silence. They had to – Ruby talked so much.

"This will be the last clue but one," she told them. "If they solve this one, they'll find the one that tells them where the treasure is." Then Ruby pulled a slip of paper from her frilly white bag and held it under Roger's nose. It said ...

In Pitt Street Park, up a tree
somewhere within THIS LAND I'll be.

"Get it?" Ruby said with a grin.

Roger shook his head.

"Good!" said Ruby. "Only the really brainy ones will get the answer."

"Can I look?" Ellie asked. Ellie looked at the paper. "Easy," she said.

Ruby's face turned an angry red. "No, it's not! There are hundreds of trees in Pitt Street Park."

"But only one on the island," Ellie said.

"How do you know it's on the island?" Ruby asked crossly.

"The clue says, 'Somewhere within THIS LAND'," Ellie said. She had worked it out. "Take the I-S from THIS and the L-A-N-D and you have I-S-L-A-N-D. Island!"

"Land ahoy!" Sniffle cried.

"Hah!" Ruby said with a nasty grin. "You only knew that because that's where we're going."

"Land a-hoyyyy!" Sniffle yelled.

"Oh no, I didn't!" Ellie told her sharply.

"Oh yes, you did!"

"Land a-HOYYYY!!" yelled Sniffle again.

"Oh no, I didn't!"

"Oh yes, you ... eeeeek!"

Ccccrrrunnnch! The *Titanic* hit the island.

"Land a-h-e-e-e-e-l-p!" Sniffle cried, as he sailed from the crow's nest and landed at the top of the island's only tree.

"Abandon ship!" Roger cried, as he climbed ashore.

"My daddy will have you punished!" Ruby cried, as green water lapped over her shiny red shoes.

"Sorry, Captain," Ellie said with a sheepish smile, as the *Titanic* sank in the shallow water.

Chapter 4
A Four-legged Parrot

Ellie lifted Sniffle down from the tree. Then Ruby gave her the treasure hunt clue. "Put that up in the tree!" she ordered.

This time Ellie didn't argue with her. She put her large hand as high up in the tree as she could reach.

Sniffle was taking bits of twig out of his nose. "How do we get back, Captain Roger?" he asked.

Roger was looking sadly at the huge hole in the *Titanic*'s side. "Swim," he said.

"I can't swim!" Sniffle told him.

"And I won't!" Ruby said and she stamped her slimy sock. "I'll just wait here till Daddy's helicopter comes to fetch me ... but you'll have to pay for the fuel," she warned.

"I guess I'll have to carry you back," Ellie said. "The water's not too deep for me."

So Ellie carried Ruby over to the shore and Roger carried Sniffle. Minnie sat on Sniffle's head.

"Mind you don't splash that smelly water on my best dress!" Ruby said. "Cost a thousand pounds in Paris, this did! And I don't think much of your dress, my dear Ellie! It's only fit to clean the floor with."

When Ellie got to the shore Ruby said, "Put me down."

Ellie turned and walked back to the edge of the lake. She put Ruby down. She put her down in the deepest, most weedy part of the lake she could find.

Ruby came up spitting out tadpoles. "You'll be hearing from my daddy!" Ruby

yelled as the Pitt Street Pirates ran off into the narrow, dusty streets. They would be safe there. They could hear Ruby wailing as she dripped towards her bike. "Oh, no! Someone's stolen my hubcaps!"

Roger panted as they ran. "We didn't get that pound off her," he said.

Ellie grinned. "Never mind. I've got something much better!" She opened her fist and waved a slip of paper under Roger's nose. "I've got the last clue to the treasure hunt. Solve the clue and get the prize! Meet me tonight in the pirates' den!"

Later that evening, Ellie switched off her TV and smiled. "That pirate in the film was doing just what pirates have to do!" she said.

"Just like my Aunty Jane," Sniffle said.

"Is your Aunty Jane a pirate?"

"No, but she does what she has to do."

"Shut up, Sniffle," Roger said with a sigh.

"Yes, Captain Roger."

"And what was that song again ... me hearty?" Captain Redbeard asked his Mate.

"Fifteen men on the dead man's chest. Yo-ho-ho and a bottle of rum," Ellie said.

Sniffle shook his head. "That song's no good for me, Captain."

"Why not?" asked Roger.

"I can't count up to fifteen. I only have ten fingers."

"You stupid land blubber ..." Roger snarled.

"Lubber!" Ellie said. "Land lubber."

"Yeah!" Roger nodded. "He's one of those, too. I'll have you talking to tanks!"

"Walking the plank," Ellie said gently.

"Yeah, that's it! Walking the plank!" Captain Redbeard turned to Ellie. "Am I starting to sound like a real pirate?" he asked.

"Oh, much better." She smiled. "And of course you're much better looking!"

"Of course," Roger agreed.

"Now all we need are the clothes," she went on. "I've made scarves for Sniffle and me."

Sniffle sniffed with joy as he saw the red spotty silk scarves. "Where did you get the silk?" he gasped.

"Mum's knickers," she said.

"Won't she miss them?"

"Not until it gets a bit colder," Ellie said.

"I'm not having knickers on my head," Roger said.

"Oh, no," Ellie told him sweetly. "I made this for you." And she pulled out a black pirate hat that just fitted Roger's head. "Now you're a real pirate captain," she said.

"Yeah!" Captain Redbeard said, as he looked at himself with pride in the cracked mirror.

He undid his shirt to the waist, kicked off his shoes and strutted up and down the room. "Are we all ready to go now?"

Ellie shook her head. "You need a parrot."

"Where will we get a parrot in Pitt Street?" Sniffle asked.

Ellie looked at Minnie the cat. All at once, her long arm shot out and she grabbed the cat. With her other hand, she tied a bit of elastic round Minnie's head and clamped a beak made of card onto her nose. She put the puzzled cat on Roger's shoulder. "Now we are a pirate crew!" she said.

"Without a ship," Sniffle pointed out.

"Ah, but with a treasure chest to find," she said. "Let's work out this last clue to Ruby Rose's treasure hunt. We'll be able to buy a hundred ships by this time tomorrow," she told them.

Chapter 5
The Crooked Cow

"I'll read the clue," Ellie said. She unfolded the grubby slip of paper that Ruby had given her to put up in the tree.

The treasure is there
if you seek deep down
in the jumbled EARTH
of the MATCHES BROWN.

"That's it!" Roger cried. "It says 'matches brown' ... the matches you can buy in Brown's shop, do you think?"

"No, I don't think so," Ellie told him.

But Roger just went on talking. "Do you know any shops owned by a Mr or Mrs Brown?" he asked Sniffle.

Sniffle blinked. "Old Bully Brown runs the Crooked Cow pub in Dock Street."

Roger punched the air. "That's it!" Then he punched his Cabin Boy on the arm. "Well done, Sniffle! Well done! Maybe you're not as stupid as you look."

Roger jumped to his feet. "We just have to dig in the earth in the back yard of the Crooked Cow!"

"No!" Ellie said. "You don't understand ..."

"Hey!" Sniffle looked scared. "That pub's a pretty tough place! They say that Baby-face Ging's gang used to hang out there in the old days. It was their hide-out."

Roger was making for the door with the cat on his shoulder. Ellie grabbed Sniffle's hand and ran after him. "Why would Ruby Rose want to hide treasure down in that part of town?" she argued.

Roger grabbed a garden trowel from a window box as he rushed out into the cool night air. "The clue is in the word 'jumbled', Roger!" Ellie tried to tell him. "It means the letters are all mixed up to make another word."

But Roger didn't hear her. He sailed on down the dark street with Ellie and Sniffle trailing behind him.

"You see," Ellie was saying, "mix up the letters in MATCHES BROWN to make new

words and you get TOWN CHAMBERS. That's
where the Town Council meets. That's where
a girl like Ruby Rose would hide the treasure.
You understand, Sniffle, don't you?"

"Er ... no, Ellie."

But Ellie went on. "The letters E-A-R-T-H
can be changed to make HEART. And the
letters in M-A-T-C-H-E-S B-R-O-W-N make
TOWN CHAMBERS. See?"

"Er … no, Ellie."

"The treasure's in the Town Chambers!" she told them.

Sniffle shook his head. "Captain Roger was right about the *Titanic*," he told her. "He'll be right this time, too."

"Yes," she said. "He's a great Captain and a fantastic ship-builder … but he's no good at word games!"

Still Roger rushed on down the dark streets muttering, "Avast and belay there, me hearties. Pieces of eight and Spanish gold!"

The tooting of the tug boats broke the silence of the dark streets as they came near the old dock area of the town.

The damp river air made Ellie shiver. The shapes in the shadows made Sniffle shake.

But bold Roger Redbeard raced on, with dreams of gold to keep out the cold.

At last he got to the high back wall of the Crooked Cow pub.

Chapter 6
Hello Ello

Minnie the cat fell off Roger's shoulder as he tried to scramble up the high brick wall. Ellie came after him. "Let me help you, Captain!" she said.

She cupped her hands and Roger put one foot in them and she lifted him up ... a little too fast. Roger shot over the wall like a cannonball and landed in the yard on his head.

He shook himself. He could hear faint sounds of laughter spilling out from the old bar. A tomcat howled close by. Minnie, the ship's parrot, howled back.

But closer still, someone moved in the shadows by the gate. "Who's that?" the bold pirate Captain hissed.

"Who's that?" a shaky voice said.

"Who's that, saying, 'Who's that?'"

"Who's that, saying, 'Who's that, saying, who's that?'" the shaky voice shook.

"I asked first," Roger Redbeard said. "Who are you?"

"Not telling," came the voice, and there was a soft, "*Sn-sn-sn-iff!*"

"Sniffle?" Roger said. "How did you get in here?"

"By the gate," the Cabin Boy replied. "It's open, you know."

Roger gave a sigh. A pirate's life is not an easy one. "Let Ellie in," he ordered. Then he began digging away at the hard earth in the corner. "You two find your own patch and let me know if you find anything."

After half an hour, Roger was up to his neck in the hole. He'd hit solid rock. He looked out. He felt stiff. The yard was silent. "Ellie?" he called.

"Aye aye, Captain?"

"Found anything?"

"Just 23 worms and 6 dog bones."

"Sniffle?"

"*Sn-sn-sn-iff?*"

"Found anything?"

"Nah. Just an old brown case."

"A brown case!" the Captain cried. "What's in it? Gold, silver and jewels?"

"No-o. Nothing like that. It's full of bits of paper. Looks like £5 notes!"

"Treasure!" Ellie and the Captain cried at once. They slammed the case shut, snatched it up and rushed out into the lane. They also rushed out into the arms of a policeman.

"Now, what have we got here?" Officer Ello asked. He took the case from the Captain's hands. "Had a report of noises in the back yard of the pub. Landlord was worried! I came round to see what was going on. You kids should be in bed at this time of night anyway."

The policeman pressed the catch of the old case and the lid sprang open. Piles of £5 notes fell out. The old policeman looked amazed. "And where did you get all this money from?"

"The back yard of the Crooked Cow pub," Ellie said sadly. "Roger worked out that it would be there."

"Did he now?" The policeman grinned. "Well, he's more clever than all the town's police! We've been looking for Baby-face Ging's loot for 25 years and have never found it."

"This is Ruby Rose's treasure hunt prize," Sniffle said.

Officer Ello smiled. "Nah! That's in the heart of the Town Chambers ... everyone knows that! All the golf club kids will end up there tomorrow. No, this is Baby-face Ging's treasure all right. And you found it. You know what this means?"

Roger gave a sigh. He was worn out. It had been a bad day. "Bad news," was all he could say.

"Hah! No, me boy! More like a reward!" The policeman grinned. "I'll just look after these £5 notes for you ... they're old notes so they aren't worth anything. You call at the Town Chambers tomorrow after lunch and I'll bet the mayor will have a big reward for you."

The policeman stuffed the money back in the case, picked it up and plodded off down the lane.

The pale light of the street lamps glinted in Ellie's adoring eyes. "Oh, Roger," she said. "You are wonderful!"

Even in the dark, Roger's cheeks glowed red.

"Avast, me hearties!" he roared. "We'll meet tomorrow in the Town Chambers."

Chapter 7
Paper Pounds

Mayor Rupert Rose blinked and put on his glasses. "Now that the Council's work is done," he said, "I can present the prizes to the finders of the treasure!"

He took an envelope out of his pocket. "In this envelope there are two tickets to America ..."

"Oh, Roger," Ellie crooned. "You and I can go away together."

The pirate Captain looked a little unhappy. "Wouldn't you rather take Sniffle?" he asked.

Ellie punched him on the arm. "Would the winners of the treasure hunt please step up here," Mayor Rupert Rose went on.

Minnie wobbled on Captain Roger's shoulder as he stepped onto the floor of the Town Chambers with Ellie and Sniffle.

The councillors gasped. The town clerk said something in the mayor's ear.

The mayor blinked again. "There seems to have been some mistake! These children found Baby-face Ging's treasure. They are not the winners of the treasure hunt!" he said.

"Ahhhh!" said all the councillors together.

The mayor looked under the table and pulled out the brown case the pirates had found.

"Of course, the notes aren't worth anything now. You can have them all back. But we'd also like to give you a token of the town's thanks!" He pushed a chest at Roger and turned to the town clerk. "Now," he said with a smile, "where's my Ruby Rose and where are the real winners of the treasure hunt?"

The Pitt Street Pirates were led out of the Town Chambers in a hurry.

It was hot outside in the street. "Open the chest, Captain Roger," Sniffle said.

Roger opened it and looked inside. Ellie took something out of the chest.

"What is it? Gold? Silver? Tickets for a holiday to America?"

Roger shook his head. Ellie held up a roll of paper. She read out ...

> **"The Town Council wishes to express its thanks to Roger Redwood and friends for finding the Ging Gang goodies.**
>
> **Signed, Rupert Rose (Mayor)"**

"They didn't even get my name right,"
Roger said as they went sadly back to Pitt
Street.

"Is that all?" Sniffle asked.

"There are one thousand useless old £5 notes. They aren't worth a penny!" Roger said, with a sigh.

"Will we build another *Titanic*?" Sniffle asked Roger as they walked past Mr Clark's shop.

Roger said nothing.

"Cheer up," Ellie said. "It could be worse."

Roger looked at her. "How? I'm a pirate who never stole anything. The treasure I found is not worth a penny. I'm a loser. How could it be worse?"

"You could be Ruby Rose!" Ellie grinned.

A bike with gold and silver trim came round the corner on just two of its three wheels. Ruby Rose was peddling like mad. "Help! Oh! Help!" she cried. "They want to kill me!"

"What's the matter, Ruby?" Ellie asked … as if she didn't know.

"The golf club kids have worked all day to follow up the clues. They went mad when they had to wade across the Pitt Street Park lake in their best clothes," Ruby said with a gasp, then looked behind her in panic.

"It was worth it to get the treasure," said Roger.

"Yes! But when they got across the lake they found the clue had gone! And they blame me!" Ruby wailed.

"How did they know where the treasure was if they never found the clue?" asked Ellie.

"Officer Ello told them. But they're still mad at me," Ruby replied.

"She's here!" a voice called out. A group of wet, muddy, angry rich kids came rushing round the corner and started to yell at Ruby Rose.

"Wahhhh!" she sobbed. "They say they're going to throw me in the lake!"

"You'll float." The Captain smiled. It was the first time he'd smiled for an hour.

"I won't float with this bike round my neck!" Ruby shouted as she pedalled on as fast as she could.

The angry golf club kids vanished round the corner after Ruby. Roger Redbeard was rolling about on the ground, laughing. Even Sniffle saw the joke.

Ellie held up a grubby slip of paper with the last clue on it. "I think this is what got lost!" She was laughing too. "Hey, Captain! Who said we couldn't rob the rich?"

"Robbing is wrong!" a shaky voice said from inside the shop. They were standing by the dusty windows of Mr Clark's shop and it was the old shopkeeper who had spoken.

The old man came to the door. "What have you got there, then?" he asked.

Roger showed him what was in the brown case. "Old £5 notes," he said, with a sigh. "Not worth a penny!"

Mr Clark looked in the box and shook his head. "Don't be stupid, lad! People collect old banknotes like those! They may not be worth £5 each but they are worth something!"

"How much?" Sniffle asked.

"A pound at least!" the old man said. "I'll give you that!"

Roger looked at Ellie and she nodded. "A pound's better than nothing," she said.

The shopkeeper took the case and went back into the gloomy shop. He came out five minutes later with a fat bundle of money. "Here you are – there were one thousand notes in there – so here's one thousand pounds for you!"

Roger could hardly speak. "I thought you said one pound!"

"One pound for each note – one thousand notes, one thousand pounds!" the old man said, and he smiled as he went slowly back into the shop.

The three pirates went on down Pitt Street in a dream. It was sunset before they woke up in the real world.

Roger sat on the warm doorstep and closed his eyes.

The houses in the street turned into great galleons in his mind. "We'll build that new galleon. We'll sail the seven seas and bring back Spanish gold!"

"What will you spend your share of the treasure on?" Ellie asked Sniffle.

"A bike," Sniffle said. "And you?"

"A new collar for Minnie," she said, stroking the pirate cat till it purred loudly.

"Then there are one or two films I want to watch," Ellie said, looking at Roger.

"Pirate films?"

Ellie shook her head. "Romantic films," she said shyly.

"Would you like to come and watch them with me, Roger?" She nudged him with her elbow.

Roger was looking across the street and seeing the great galleons in his mind. "I'll buy a new ship – a real sailing ship. It'll be the best on the seven seas."

"What'll you call it?" Ellie asked. "*The Fair Ellie?*"

Roger shook his head. "No-o," he said. "The first ship led us to the treasure. It was a lucky ship for us. Yes. I'll call my new ship *Titanic Two* … I can't help thinking that's a lucky name for a ship!"

Our books are tested
for children and young people by
children and young people.

Thanks to everyone who consulted on
a manuscript for their time and effort in
helping us to make our books better
for our readers.

More **4u2read** titles ...

All Sorts to Make a World

JOHN AGARD

Shona's day has been packed with characters. First there was 3.2-million-year-old Lucy in the Natural History Museum, and then Pinstripe Man, Kindle Woman, Doctor Bananas and the iPod Twins.

Now Shona and her dad are on a Tube train that's stuck in a tunnel and everyone around them is going ... bananas!

The Hat Trick

TERRY DEARY

A game of two halves ...

Jud's team is 2–0 down in the big match when their star player is hurt.

Can Jud save the day?

Mozart's Banana

GILLIAN CROSS

Mozart's Banana – a crazy name for a crazy horse.

No one can tame Mozart's Banana. Even Sammy Foster failed, and he reckons he's the boss of the school. Mozart's Banana is just too crazy.

But then Alice Brett turns up. Alice is as cool as a choc-ice, and she isn't going to let anyone get the better of her, horse or boy ...

The Black Knight of Gressingham

PHILIP ARDAGH

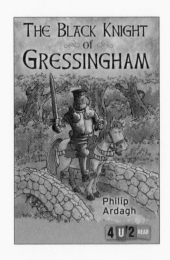

Squat is off to join the Green Men of Gressingham. The Green Men are outlaws. They live in the forest and do brave deeds.

The Green Men have a special task for Squat. He must fight nasty Sir Jack de Zack.

But how can tiny Squat beat big, strong Sir Jack? Worry not! The Green Men have a *plan*. And also a *cabbage*.

www.barringtonstoke.co.uk